To Reach the Top

Clare La Plante

STECK-VAUGHN
ELEMENTARY · SECONDARY · ADULT · LIBRARY

A Harcourt Company

www.steck-vaughn.com

ISBN 0-7398-5101-2

Contents

Tenzing Norgay and Edmund Hillary reached the top of Mount Everest in 1953.

CHAPTER ONE

Why People Climb Mountains

It was May 1953. Two men were climbing a dangerous cliff. They were thousands of feet high, halfway up the world's tallest mountain.

The mountain was Everest. It is 29,035 feet tall. That's an **altitude** of almost five and a half miles. It is almost as high as twenty Empire State Buildings stacked on top of each other.

The two men were alone. If they fell, no one would hear their screams. Their lives depended on a rope that tied them together. The men attached the rope to hooks they pounded into the frozen mountain.

Suddenly, the bigger man, Edmund Hillary, stepped on a loose chunk of ice. It broke. He fell off the mountain. The smaller man, Tenzing Norgay, braced himself.

The rope tugged him hard, but he was strong. With Hillary hanging below, Norgay took a deep breath. He pulled Hillary back up.

Why would two men **risk** their lives like this? Hillary and Norgay wanted to be the first to climb to the top of Mount Everest. No one had ever done it.

Did You Know?

Legend says that a large creature with four toes and red hair lives on Mount Everest. It is half man, half beast. People in the area, the Sherpas, call it "Yeti." English-speaking people call it "The Abominable Snowman."

Two Brave Men

Hillary and Norgay began their **expedition** three months earlier. It started with almost 400 people helping them. These other people helped carry supplies. They also set up camps along the 175 miles of trails that led up Mount Everest.

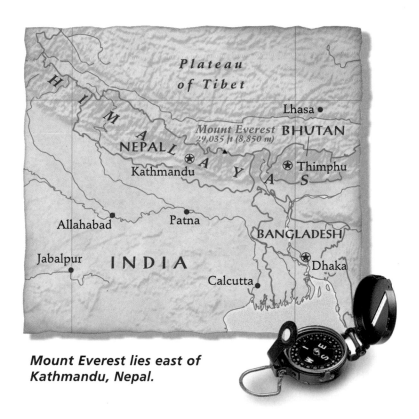

Mount Everest lies east of Kathmandu, Nepal.

Hillary was a shy man from New Zealand who longed for adventure. He loved to climb mountains.

Norgay was a Sherpa who grew up near Mount Everest. Sherpas are mountain people from the country of Nepal. Norgay loved to climb, too. He worked as a guide in the Himalayas, the mountain range where Mount Everest is.

In the forty or so years before Hillary and Norgay's trip, climbers from ten other expeditions had already tried to reach the **summit** of Mount Everest. They had failed. Nineteen men had died, and two had disappeared.

Norgay and Hillary were determined to reach the peak. In fact, Norgay said that he would reach the top "or die."

By May 28, 1953, Norgay and Hillary had left their helpers behind. The two spent the night alone in a frozen tent 27,900 feet above sea level. It was the highest place that anyone had ever camped.

The next morning, at 4:00 A.M., they ate a breakfast of **sardines** and melted snow with lemon and sugar. Then they began the final stretch of the climb.

Each man wore eight layers of clothes and carried forty pounds of equipment. They moved carefully. They were in the Death Zone.

This **zone** is a dangerous area that starts at 25,000 feet. The air is "thin" there—it does not have much **oxygen**. Hillary and Norgay had to use oxygen masks in order to breathe.

The air is also very cold. It can be one hundred degrees below **zero** on Mount Everest. The wind was so fierce, it could knock the men off their feet.

Hillary and Norgay struggled up the mountain. Suddenly, Norgay couldn't breathe. At first, neither man knew why. Then Hillary saw that ice had blocked Norgay's oxygen line. Quickly, Hillary fixed the blocked line.

Soon the men saw the mountain's peak. To reach it, they would have to climb a thin ledge. To one side of the ledge, there was a drop of 8,000 feet. To the other side, the drop **increased** to 10,000 feet. If either man fell, he would die.

Taking one step at a time, they made it to the top. Hillary and Norgay had reached the highest place on Earth! They hugged each other to celebrate their **triumph**. Norgay thanked the mountain by leaving some chocolate in the snow. Hillary left a small cross.

What did they see on top of the world? "Nothing above us, a world below," Edmund Hillary said.

Mount Everest is 29,035 feet tall.

Why Climb Mountains?

Many people like Hillary and Norgay have risked their lives to climb mountains. Why do they do this?

Some people climb mountains to explore. They want to learn more about nature or themselves. Many like the challenge of doing something dangerous.

When asked why people climb mountains, a famous mountain climber named George Mallory had an answer. He said that people will climb a mountain "because it is there."

CHAPTER TWO

Training and Equipment

Mountain climbing is not a sport like baseball or football. You don't play against another team. You don't keep score.

You need to be in good shape to climb a mountain, just as you do in other sports. Mountain climbers need to have strong bodies and minds.

In mountain climbing, you **compete** against ice, snow, and rocks. You also battle against the altitude. If you want to become a climber, you will need to prepare yourself. You can start by training your body.

Training

First, you must build up your **stamina**. If you have stamina, you can exercise for a long time without getting tired. You need stamina for other sports, too, such as football and basketball.

Another important part of training is to **strengthen** your heart and lungs. You can make your heart and lungs stronger by running, biking, or climbing stairs.

One mountain climber trained by climbing forty flights of stairs ten times each morning. That's 400 flights of stairs every day! He took the elevator down between climbs.

Finally, you need to learn how to use climbing equipment. If you want to climb high mountains, you'll need to learn how to tie knots in a rope and how to use an ice ax. You also should learn how to set up a tent and make water from snow.

You can't learn how to do all this on the mountain. You must learn before you go.

Mountain Climbing Equipment

Before you start climbing, it's important to get the right equipment. You may want to take classes to learn how to use it correctly.

Your climbing equipment can mean the difference between life and death. Here is a list of everything you'll need:

✓ **Ice ax** You can use an ax like a cane or to carve stairs into the ice. You also can use it to stop yourself from falling down a mountain by digging the pick part of the ax into the ice or snow.

✓ **Boots with spikes** These will keep your feet warm and dry. The spikes attach to your boots. These will help you walk on the ice.

✓ **Waterproof clothing** This clothing protects you against rain and snow. It should help keep you warm and dry.

✓ **Backpack** Your backpack can carry everything from food and clothes to your sleeping bag and tent.

✓ **Stove** A stove can be used to melt snow into drinking water. You also can use it to cook soup and other instant food, such as rice and potatoes.

✓ **Compass, map, and two-way radio** The compass and map will help you find the right way. You can use the two-way radio to call for help if you get lost.

✓ **Flashlight** You may choose to carry a flashlight or to wear one on your head like a person who works in mines. Your flashlight can help you see in the dark or in a windy snowstorm like a **blizzard**.

✓ **Metal spikes and clamps** You use these tools to attach ropes to the mountain as you climb.

✓ **Ropes** You can use rope to tie yourself to another climber, as Norgay and Hillary did. You can also attach rope to the mountain to help you climb.

✓ **Oxygen mask and tank** These will give you extra oxygen during higher climbs. If you climb tall mountains without extra oxygen, you are three times more likely to die.

✓ **Sun block and dark glasses** Sunblock will protect you from getting serious burns. The glasses will keep the sun's **ultraviolet** rays from harming your eyes.

✓ **First-aid kit** Your kit should include medicine and bandages. ⚡

Ice ax

Waterproof
clothing

Rope

Boots
with spikes

Your Climbing Team

When Hillary and Norgay climbed Everest, they started with almost 400 people. Today, expeditions are smaller.

Some people go by themselves, but this is very unsafe. Other people go in groups of about three to ten. As a beginning climber, you should always go with a group.

For hard mountain climbs, you might choose to hire guides. The guides on Mount Everest are often Sherpas. Sherpas are **accustomed** to breathing the thinner mountain air.

Sherpas are also strong and can carry large backpacks filled with equipment. Many other guides won't carry supplies, but you can hire them to lead you up and down a mountain.

Whether you hire a guide or go with your friends, family, or a climbing club, you should always be prepared.

You must be prepared for anything when you climb a mountain.

CHAPTER THREE

Tragedies, Triumphs, and Amazing Stories

Like other high-risk sports, climbing has its share of **tragedies**. Since the 1920s, more than 160 people have died trying to climb Mount Everest.

On Annapurna, another tall mountain in the Himalaya Mountains, more than fifty people have died. When a climber dies, other climbers usually leave the body on the mountain. Pulling a body down a mountain is too dangerous.

In the spring of 1996, there was an **unexpected** blizzard on Mount Everest. Eight climbers died in three days.

The climbers couldn't see where they were going. Some walked off the edge of the mountain. The bodies of others were found just a few feet from their tents.

Another **disaster** took place in the 1800s. Edward Whymper was an English painter. He wanted to be the first person to climb the Matterhorn, a tall mountain in Switzerland.

On his eighth try, Whymper made it to the top with six other men. The seven climbers tied themselves together with rope.

Suddenly, one climber slipped off the mountain. Three others fell with him. All four climbers died.

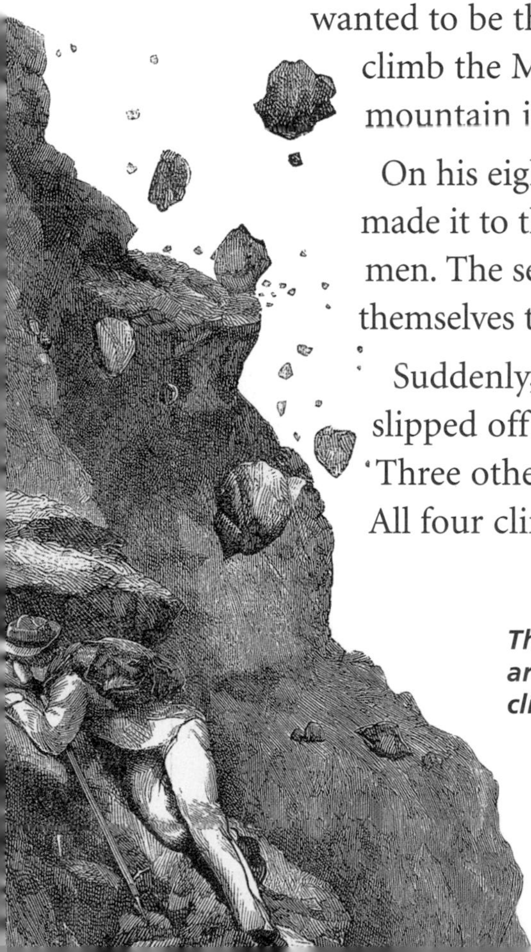

This picture shows an artist's idea of Whymper climbing the Matterhorn.

Later, people wondered why Whymper and the other climbers hadn't fallen, too. After all, they were tied to the same rope as the men who fell. Whymper claimed the rope broke. Other people said he cut it to save his own life. No one will ever know what really happened.

Triumphs

In May 2001, Erik Weihenmayer climbed to the top of Mount Everest. His climb was a triumph for climbers everywhere, but especially for people who are blind.

Weihenmayer was born with an eye **disease**. When he was 13 years old, he went blind. He began climbing mountains when he was in his early 20s.

How did Weihenmayer climb Everest? He had special equipment to help him. He listened to bells attached to his fellow climbers. His fellow climbers would call out directions. "Death Fall two feet to your right!" Weihenmayer's climb gave hope to others with disabilities who would like to climb.

Erik Weihenmayer receives a banner from the National Federation of the Blind.

Twenty-year-old Keegan Reilly could not use his legs. He had been **paralyzed** in a car accident. Reilly climbed a mountain in Colorado named Mount Elbert. He used a special chair. It took him four days. He said reaching the top was one of the greatest moments of his life.

In 1911, women in America couldn't vote. Few women were climbing mountains. Annie Smith Peck climbed Mount Coropuna in Peru and planted a *Votes for Women* flag on the summit. She was 61 years old. Annie Smith Peck saw women win the right to vote in 1920. At the age of 82, she was still climbing mountains.

Annie Smith Peck climbed mountains when it was unusual for a woman to do so.

Amazing Stories

Some of the most amazing climbing stories arc storics of **survival**. In 1996, Dr. Beck Weathers was left for dead in the snow on Mount Everest.

His teammates thought that he had frozen to death. He was too heavy to carry back to camp. They left him. Weathers lay on the icy ground all night.

In the morning, Weathers woke up and stumbled back into camp. When members of his expedition team saw him, they thought that he had come back from the dead!

Weathers **survived**, although he lost some fingers and his nose to the cold.

Other climbing stories don't end so happily. George Mallory was a famous climber. In 1924, he disappeared while making the climb up Mount Everest. At that time, nobody knew what had happened to him.

Seventy-five years later, in 1999, climbers found Mallory's body near the top of Mount Everest. The icy temperatures that had killed him had also preserved his body.

The ice **preserved** Mallory's body so well that he looked very much as he had in 1924. His clothes looked almost new. He was still holding on to the mountain.

Though Mallory has been found, people still have many questions about him. Was he climbing up or coming back down Mount Everest when he died? Could he have been the first man to climb Everest? No one knows.

When Mallory started his climb, he had a camera with him. It hasn't been found yet. If it is found, experts say the film can still be developed. Maybe then we will learn more about what happened to George Mallory so many years ago. ⚡

Mallory, standing second from the left, poses for a picture on his 1924 climb of Mount Everest.

CHAPTER FOUR

How to Handle Emergencies

Mountain climbing can be a fun, exciting sport. It can also be very dangerous. Before you set off to climb a mountain, make sure that you are well prepared.

Being well prepared means more than having the right equipment. It means training hard until you have good stamina and a strong body. You should also prepare your mind for the journey ahead. Then you'll be ready to face the climb.

Smart climbers know that being prepared doesn't mean you won't get hurt. Remember that it isn't wise to take **risks**.

Don't climb if the weather is supposed to be bad. Don't start a climb if you feel too tired.

Of course, even the best-prepared climbers have problems. You might just be in the wrong place at the wrong time. That's why it's important to know what to do in an emergency.

Mountain Emergencies

One emergency that can happen while you're climbing is called mountain sickness. Mountain sickness is caused by being in a high altitude. The higher you climb up a mountain, the thinner the air becomes. This means there is less oxygen to breathe.

If you get mountain sickness, your head may start to hurt. You might feel so dizzy that you fall down. You may have trouble sleeping. Mountain sickness can get so bad that it makes your brain swell. It can even cause your lungs to fill with water. If this happens, you could die.

Here are some tips to prevent mountain sickness. When you start to climb, go slowly until your body gets accustomed to the thinner air. ☃

Make sure that you have emergency medicine with you. There is a special medicine you can take for mountain sickness.

Drink water to help your lungs. They must work harder at high altitudes. If these tips don't help, do the smart thing. Return to the bottom of the mountain right away.

Another climbing emergency is **frostbite**. Frostbite happens when part of your body gets so cold that it becomes frozen. With frostbite, you could lose toes, fingers, or even your nose!

If you get frostbite, warm the frozen skin as soon as possible. One way to do this is to bathe the skin in warm water, but be careful! If the water is too hot, it could harm your skin even more.

Mountain Sickness and Your Body

16,000–19,000 Feet

Your blood has one-third less oxygen here. You can't breathe well. You feel dizzy. You may not be able to sleep.

20,000–25,000 Feet

You are breathing four times faster than you usually do. You may get a very bad cough. You might start to have strange dreams or see things. You won't think very clearly. You may start to slow down.

Above 25,000 Feet

This is the Death Zone. Things go from bad to worse. You may be careless. You get so tired that you can walk only ten steps before falling over. You will also get very cold because the lack of oxygen makes it hard to get warm enough. Even if you survive, your memory may never be as sharp.

After warming the skin, try not to move the body part. Keep the area warm, dry, and clean. Of course, you should also see a doctor as soon as you can.

A third emergency is an **avalanche**. An avalanche happens when new snow falls on top of old snow. The new snow doesn't stick, so it slides down the mountain.

What to Do in an Emergency

Emergency	Symptoms	What to do
Altitude/mountain sickness	You may have a headache, dizziness, trouble sleeping, or confusion.	Climb slowly to get used to the height, have medicine in case you get sick, drink a lot of water, and go back down right away if you get very sick.
Frostbite	Skin turns white, gets numb, or may form blisters. Your skin may swell, itch, or burn as it warms.	Warm the skin as soon as possible. Use warm, not hot, water. Try not to move the body part. See a doctor as soon as you can.
Avalanche		Stay calm, close your mouth, take off your backpack, swim with the rushing snow, stay near the surface.
Whiteout		Dig a hole in the snow. Don't leave the hole until the whiteout is over.

If you are in an avalanche, try to stay calm as the snow rushes toward you. Close your mouth to keep from choking on the snow. Then take off your backpack and begin "swimming" with the rushing snow.

Try to swim in the same direction that the snow is flowing. Stay as close as possible to the snow's surface. ⚡

A **whiteout** is another emergency that snow causes on a mountain. In a whiteout, a blizzard or snow fog makes everything look white. You can't tell the difference between the sky and the ground.

Never climb a mountain during a whiteout. If you're already climbing, stop and dig a hole in the snow. Don't leave the hole until the whiteout is over.

If you follow these tips, you are more likely to stay safe in a climbing emergency.

CHAPTER FIVE

Climbing Today and in the Future

Mountain climbing has changed a lot over the years. Years ago, only a few people climbed mountains. These were usually expert climbers. Most of those people were men. Today, many people climb mountains. Women, kids, and people with **physical** challenges are climbers.

In the past, climbers raced to be the first to climb the mighty Mount Everest. Today, more than 1,000 people have made it to the top of Mount Everest!

Did You Know?

Maury McKinney teaches mountain climbing. Some of the best climbers he's ever seen are middle-school girls.

In one year alone, 1,305 people tried to climb Alaska's Mount McKinley, also called Denali. Mount McKinley is the highest mountain in the United States. More than half of the people who tried to climb Mount McKinley made it.

Many climbers today are **novices**. Their lack of experience makes climbing even more dangerous. With all these climbers, mountains can get fairly crowded.

Sometimes you have to wait your turn to climb up a narrow path. You might wait too long and run out of oxygen.

Mountain climbing today has its problems, but many things have also improved. Some of the best changes have been in equipment.

Today, oxygen tanks weigh only twenty pounds. When Hillary and Norgay climbed Mount Everest, their oxygen tanks weighed about thirty pounds each.

Other things have improved as well. Climbers used to climb in leather boots. Ice clung to these boots whenever they got wet. Imagine how hard it would be to walk in icy boots on flat ground. Now imagine climbing a mountain in cold, icy boots.

Climbers now have light, waterproof boots. Clothes, ropes, and tents are also made to be light and waterproof.

Today's climbers also get help from new **technology**. Pictures taken from space show clear paths on mountains.

Climbers can use these pictures to learn the safest places to climb. Some climbers even bring computers on their journey. The group that found Mallory's body was shown live on the Internet.

Technology also gives climbers quicker and easier ways to get to the base of a mountain. Today, many climbers travel by helicopter. In the past, climbers had to walk many miles just to get to the base of a mountain. ⚡

New Challenges

Today, many climbers have climbed the tallest mountains in the world. Now they are looking for new climbing adventures.

The Highest Summit on Each Continent

Continent	Mountain	Height Feet	Meters
Asia	Everest	29,035	8,850
South America	Aconcagua	22,834	6,960
North America	McKinley (Denali)	20,320	6,194
Africa	Kilimanjaro	19,340	5,995
Europe	Elbrus	18,510	5,642
Antarctica	Vinson Massif	16,066	4,897
Australia	Kosciusko	7,310	2,228

One new challenge is to take harder paths. Climbers have found many different ways to climb Mount Everest.

Some climbers like the challenge of doing good **deeds** during a climb. These climbers might clean up mountains, collecting garbage left by other climbers. Other climbers climb to raise money for groups who help people with diseases.

Another new challenge is climbing **remote** mountains. Remote mountains are located far from where people live. The climbers might be the only people around. This increases their risk, because it could take longer to be rescued in an emergency.

Mount Olympus on Mars is taller than any mountain on Earth.

Another World

What will happen when all the mountains on Earth have been climbed? Some people may imagine climbing on Mars. There is a mountain on Mars called Mount Olympus that is higher than Mount Everest.

If you climbed on Mars, you could carry a lot of equipment. The force of **gravity** there is weaker than on Earth. One hundred pounds on Mars is equal to 38 pounds on Earth.

But there would be problems, too. Temperatures on Mars can drop to 130 degrees below zero. You'd need extra-heavy clothes and a thick sleeping bag to keep you warm. You would also need special glasses to protect you from the **intense** ultraviolet light.

Mountain climbing on Mars is still a dream for the future. For now, people will continue to climb mountains here on Earth. As long as there are mountains, people will climb.

Glossary

accustomed (uh KUHS tuhmd) *adjective* Accustomed means used to something.

altitude (AL tuh tood) *noun* Altitude tells how high something is above sea level.

avalanche (AV uh lanch) *noun* An avalanche is a large body of snow or rock that rushes down a mountain.

blizzard (BLIHZ uhrd) *noun* A blizzard is a bad storm with heavy winds and snow.

clamps (KLAMPS) *noun* Clamps are tools that hold something in place.

compass (KUHM puhs) *noun* A compass is a tool that is used for showing direction.

compete (kuhm PEET) *verb* To compete is to fight or struggle against another person or against a thing.

deeds (DEEDZ) *noun* Deeds are people's acts.

disaster (dih ZAS tuhr) *noun* A disaster is a sudden event that causes a lot of harm.

disease (dih ZEEZ) *noun* A disease is a sickness.

expedition (ek spuh DIH shuhn) *noun* An expedition is a trip taken for a special reason.

frostbite (FRAWST byt) *noun* Frostbite is harm that happens because a body part dies of cold.

gravity (GRAV uh tee) *noun* Gravity is the force that pulls two bodies together, such as you and the earth. It is gravity that causes objects to have weight.

increased (ihn KREEST) *verb* Increased means became greater.

intense (ihn TEHNS) *adjective* Intense describes something that is very, very strong.

novices (NAHV ihs uhz) *noun* Novices are people who are new at something.

oxygen (AHK sih juhn) *noun* Oxygen is an invisible gas in the air that people need to breathe.

paralyzed (PAIR uh lyzd) *adjective* To be paralyzed is to be made not able to move a body part.

physical (FIZ ih kuhl) *adjective* Physical means having to do with the body.

preserved (pree ZURVD) *verb* Preserved means kept something from spoiling or from harm.

remote (rih MOHT) *adjective* Remote means far away from other things.

risk (RIHSK) *verb* To risk something is to take a chance of losing that thing.

risks (RIHSKS) *noun* Risks are actions people do that have some danger for the people who do them.

sardines (sahr DEENZ) *noun* Sardines are a kind of small fish.

spikes (SPYKS) *noun* Spikes are pointed metal objects used to keep people or ropes from slipping.

stamina (STAM uh nuh) *noun* Stamina is the strength to keep going.

strengthen (STREHNGTH uhn) *verb* To strengthen is to make stronger.

summit (SUHM iht) *noun* The summit is the highest point of a mountain.

survival (sur VY vuhl) *noun* Survival is the act of living through an event.

survived (sur VYVD) *verb* Survived means lived through an event.

technology (tehk NAHL uh jee) *noun* Technology is the use of science to solve everyday problems.

tragedies (TRAJ uh deez) *noun* Tragedies are very sad events.

triumph (TRY umf) *noun* A triumph is a win or a success.

ultraviolet (uhl truh VY uh liht) *adjective* Ultraviolet describes a kind of light that people cannot see. It is harmful to the eyes and skin.

unexpected (uhn ihk SPEK tuhd) *adjective* Unexpected means not expected.

whiteout (WYT owt) *noun* A whiteout is a weather event in which blowing snow makes everything look white and makes it hard for people to see.

zero (ZEE roh) *noun* Zero is the point that lies one degree below one on a temperature scale.

zone (ZOHN) *noun* A zone is an area that is set off from other areas.

Index